Little Rabbits'
First Word Book

Alan Baker

KING*f*ISHER

NEW YORK

Clothes

shoes

cap

jacket

shirt

socks

buttons

underpants

dress

sweater

pants

rain
boots

vest

3

In the kitchen

cup

plate

saucer

teapot

mug

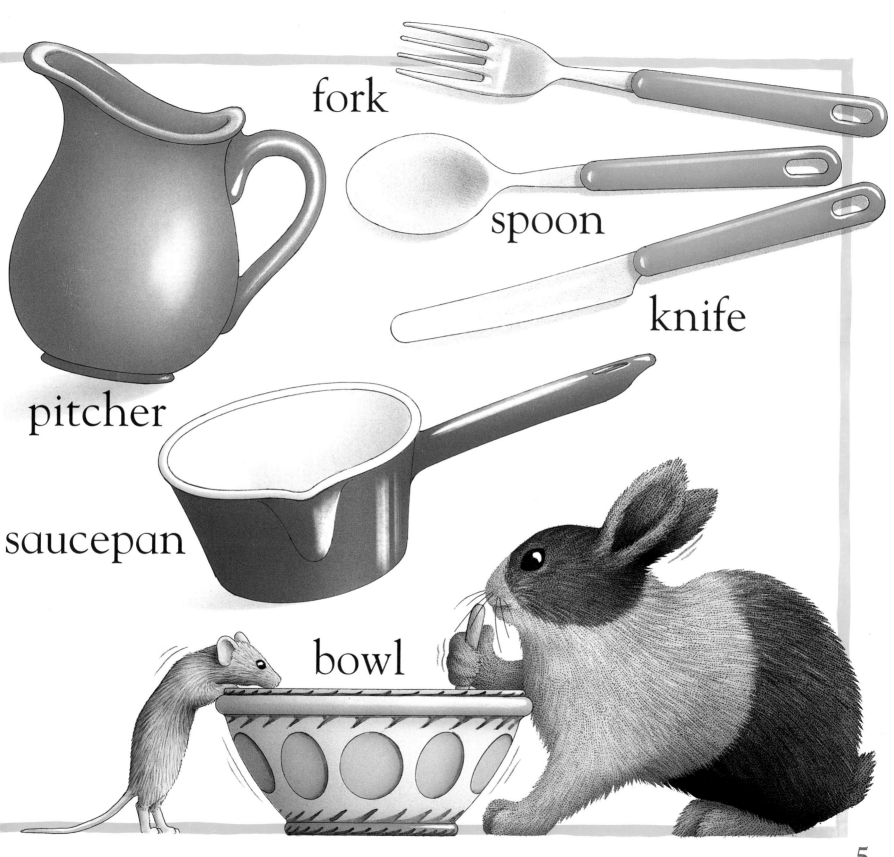

fork

spoon

knife

pitcher

saucepan

bowl

5

Toys

telephone

doll

wagon

blocks

6

rattle

puzzle

beads

cards

train

7

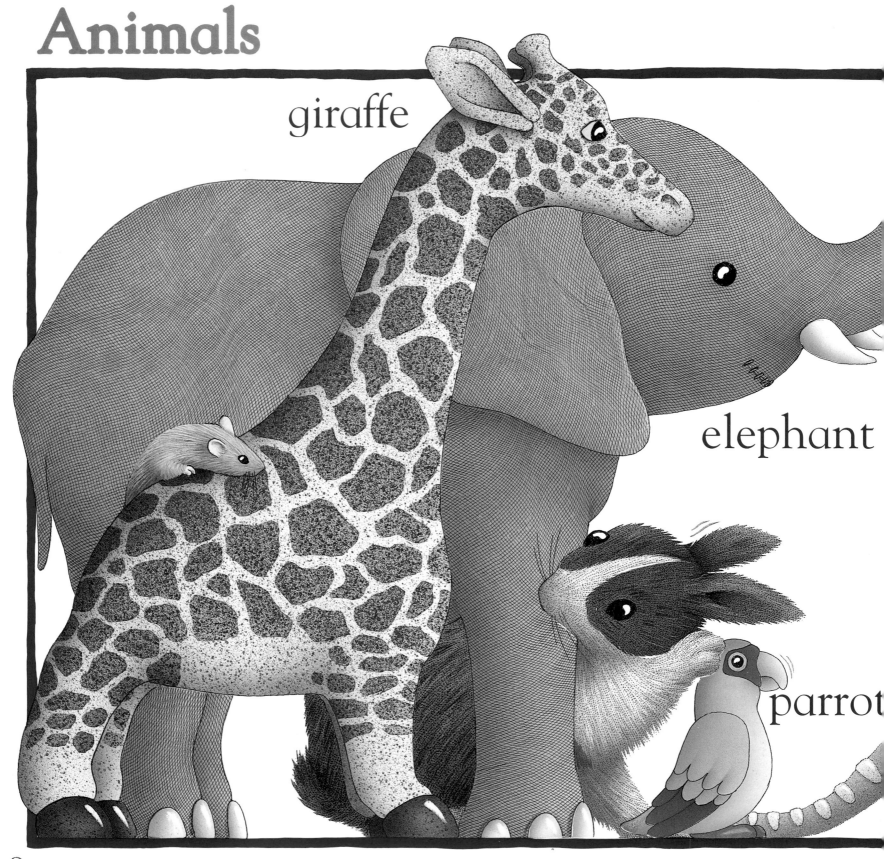

Animals

giraffe

elephant

parrot

8

tiger

monkey

crocodile

kangaroo

lion

panda

zebra

snake

9

Around the house

cushion

books

keys

dustpan

broom

brush

picture

lamp

vase

chair

table

11

Making a noise

whistle

recorder

drum

flute

tambourine

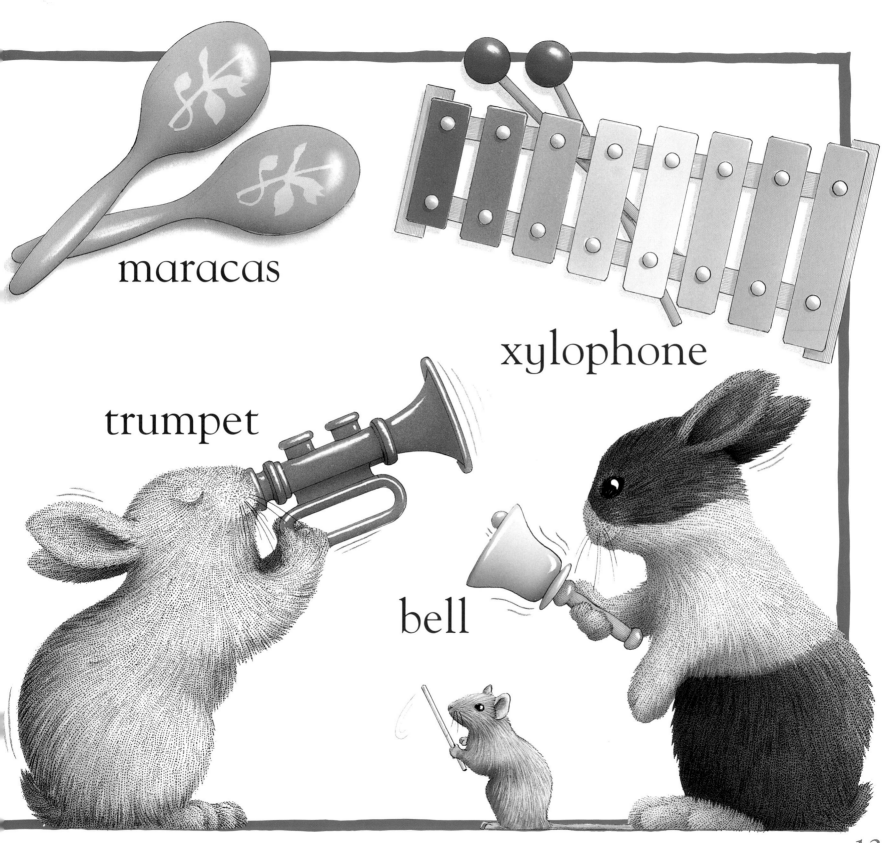

maracas

xylophone

trumpet

bell

Drawing and painting

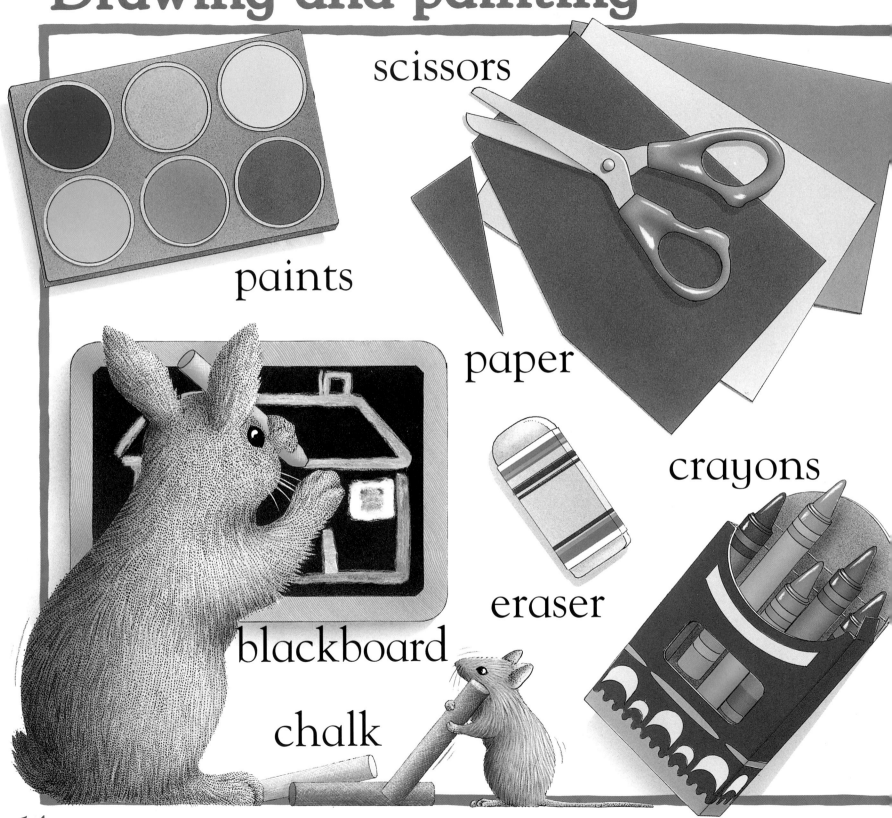

paints

scissors

paper

crayons

eraser

blackboard

chalk

ruler

felt-tip pens

paintbrushes

pencil

easel

15

Colors

yellow

blue

red

black

lemon

strawberries

beetle

butterfly

pumpkin

purple

brown

green

orange

rabbit

frog

grapes

17

Shapes

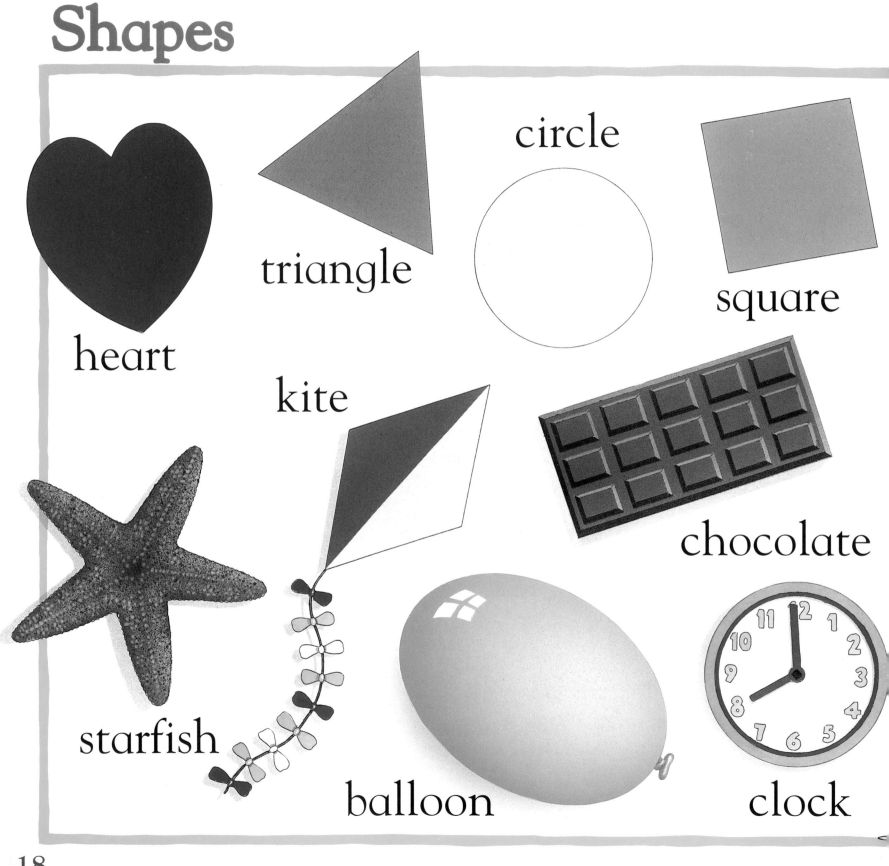

heart

triangle

circle

square

kite

chocolate

starfish

balloon

clock

diamond

oval

rectangle

star

washcloth

valentine

flags

19

At the park

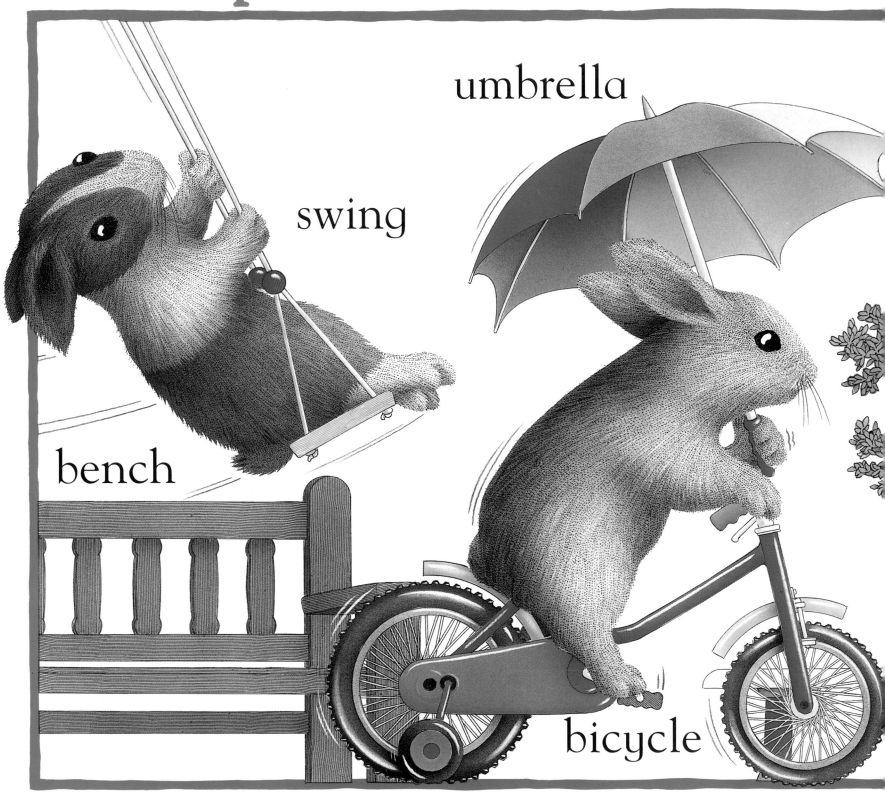

swing

umbrella

bench

bicycle

tree

slide

seesaw

21

Things to eat

cookies

sandwich

apple

banana

carrots

cheese

orange

noodles

corn

tomato

yogurt

lettuce

ice cream

On the farm

pig

chicks

horse

cow

goat

rooster

dog

duck

hen

sheep

tractor

25

Bathtime

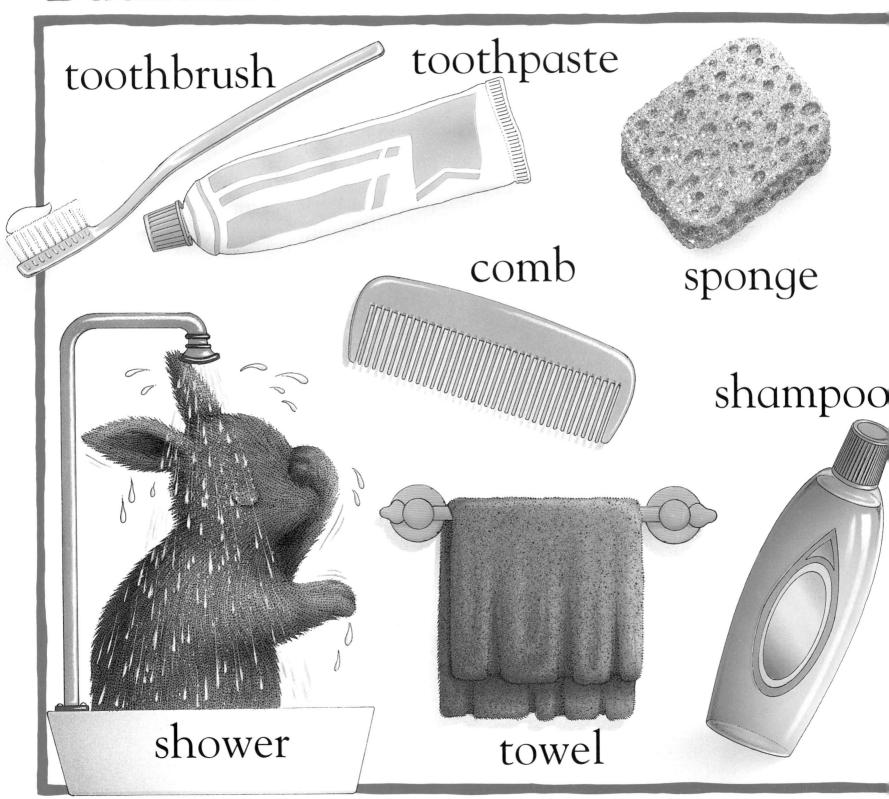

toothbrush

toothpaste

sponge

comb

shampoo

shower

towel

hairbrush

bubbles

soap

talcum
powder

mirror

bathtub

Bedtime

quilt

slippers

bathrobe

blanket

28

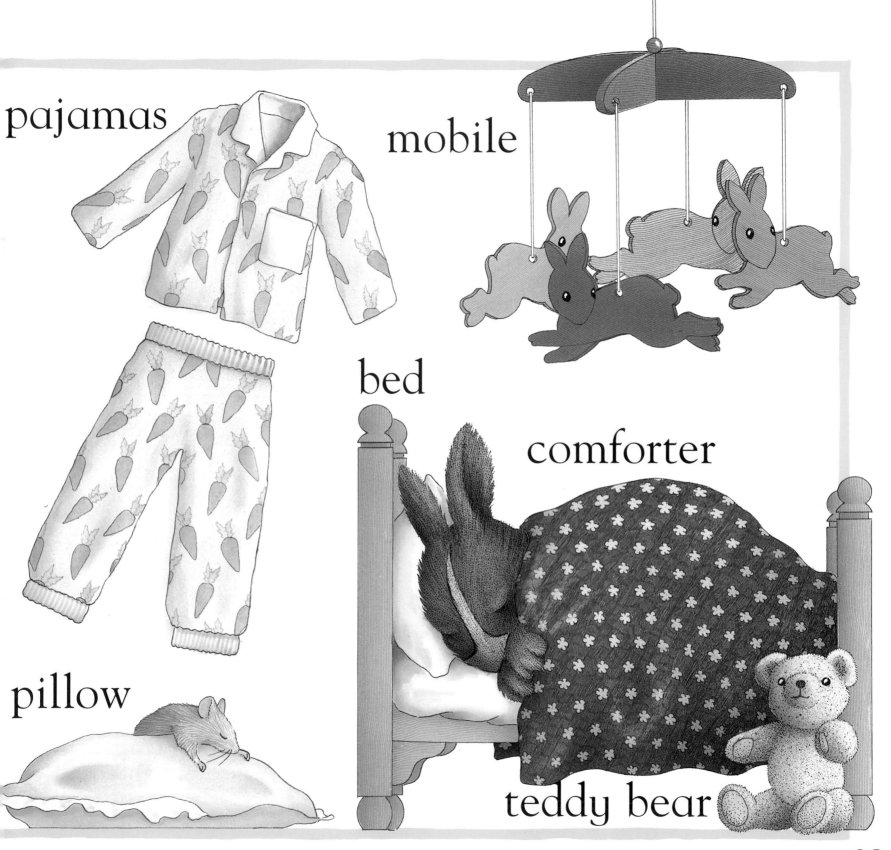

pajamas

mobile

bed

comforter

pillow

teddy bear

29

Games to play

Playing these games with your child makes learning to recognize colors and shapes more fun. They will help develop observation as well as verbal, sorting, and matching skills.

Where's the mouse?
Ask your child to look for the little brown mouse that appears in every scene. Help him or her to describe what the mouse is doing.

Who says moo? (pages 24-25)
Very young children love identifying and imitating animal noises. See if your child can find the animal to match the noises you make. Alternatively, point to an animal and ask your child to make the right noise.

Color match (pages 16-17)
Ask your child to say what is blue on these pages. Continue through the other six colors, matching each brushstroke to the fruit or animal of the same color.

Shape match (pages 18-19)
Help your child to find an object to match each of the two-dimensional shapes shown at the top of these pages. Introduce the names of some of the shapes.

What is round?
Help your child to look for round shapes or circles on some pages. Examples are: buttons (page 2), plate (page 4), beads, train wheels (pages 6-7), tambourine (page 12), paint box colors (page 14), circle and clock (page 18), wheels (page 20), bubbles (page 27).

Big and little (pages 8-9)
Ask your child which is the biggest animal and which is the smallest in this scene. Extend the discussion to other characteristics, for example: Who can fly? Who has stripes? Who can jump?

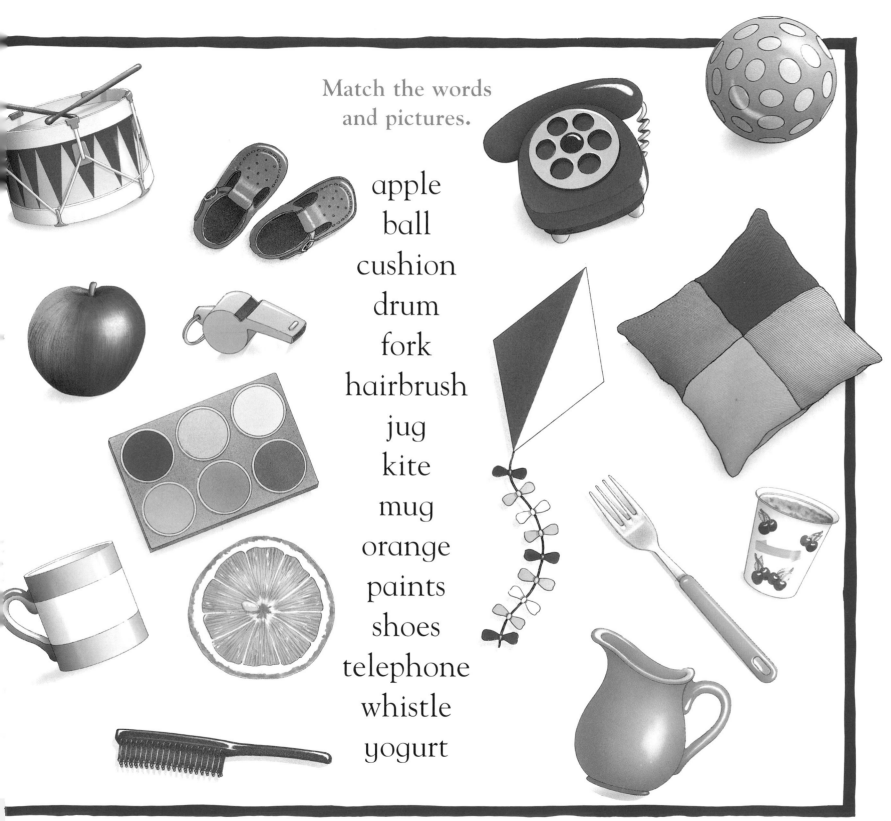

Match the words
and pictures.

apple
ball
cushion
drum
fork
hairbrush
jug
kite
mug
orange
paints
shoes
telephone
whistle
yogurt

Note to parents

This book contains a wealth of beautiful illustrations showing familiar objects that young children will enjoy identifying.

You will also find numerous opportunities to introduce concepts such as color, shape, and number. You can help to reinforce your child's early learning skills by playing some of the games suggested on pages 30-31.

Talking about pictures is an excellent way to help your child develop verbal fluency and a rich vocabulary. By drawing attention to favorite words, you can introduce the idea of printed language. Encourage your child to look at the details in the pictures. This visual skill will be important later for learning to read.

Remember—always go at your child's pace and give constant praise. Your help and encouragement will enable your child to make the most of the learning experiences this book has to offer.

KINGFISHER
Larousse Kingfisher Chambers Inc.
80 Maiden Lane
New York, New York 10038
www.kingfisherpub.com

First published in hardcover in 1996
First published in paperback in 2001
2 4 6 8 10 9 7 5 3 1

1TR / 0501 / TWP / PW / NYM150

LIBRARY OF CONGRESS CATALOGING-IN-PUBLICATION DATA
Baker, Alan.
Little Rabbits' first word book / Alan Baker—1st ed.
p. cm.
Summary: Rabbits present words and matching pictures grouped under such topics as toys, food, things that move, animals, and drawing and painting. Includes simple word and concept games.
1. Vocabulary—juvenile literature [1. Vocabulary] I. Title.
PE1449.B29 1996
428.1—dc20 96-7359 CIP AC

ISBN 0-7534-5355-X

Printed in Singapore